MINI CLASSICS

BRER RABBIT
AND THE
RIDING HORSE
And Other Stories

RETOLD BY STEPHANIE LASLETT
ILLUSTRATED BY STEPHEN HOLMES

||| •PARRAGON• |||

TITLES IN SERIES I AND II OF THE MINI CLASSICS INCLUDE:

SERIES I

Aladdin and the Magic Lamp
Ali Baba and the Forty Thieves
Alice in Wonderland
A Child's Garden of Verses
Cinderella
The Emperor's New Clothes
The Frog Prince
Goldilocks and the Three Bears
Hansel and Grettel
The Happy Prince
The Little Mermaid
Mother Goose's Rhymes
The Owl and the Pussycat (and other Nonsense Verse)
Puss in Boots
Sleeping Beauty
Snow White and the Seven Dwarfs
The Town Mouse and the Country Mouse (and other
  Aesop's Fables)
The Three Little Pigs
The Ugly Duckling
The Wizard of Oz

SERIES II

Beauty and the Beast
Brer Rabbit and Brer Fox
A Christmas Carol
The Hare and the Tortoise
How the Leopard Got His Spots
Jack and the Beanstalk
The Magic Carpet
The Night Before Christmas
Pinocchio
Rapunzel
Red Riding Hood
The Secret Garden
The Selfish Giant
Sinbad the Sailor
The Snow Queen
The Steadfast Tin Soldier
Thumbelina
The Walrus and the Carpenter
The Wind in the Willows I
The Wind in the Willows II

For Tom and Olive — SH

For Gareth — SL

A Parragon Book

Published by
Parragon Books,
Unit 13-17, Avonbridge Trading Estate,
Atlantic Road, Avonmouth, Bristol BS11 9QD

Produced by
The Templar Company plc,
Pippbrook Mill, London Road, Dorking, Surrey RH4 1JE

Designed by Mark Kingsley-Monks

Printed and bound in Great Britain

ISBN 1-85813-805-1

Many years ago on a big cotton plantation down in the deep south of North America there lived an old black slave called Uncle Remus. Every evening as the sun set behind the persimmon trees and the shadows lengthened across the dusty yard, Uncle Remus would sit in a creaky old rocking chair on

the verandah, light his pipe
and tell his tales to anyone
who would care to listen.
If the children were good
and quiet then they could
listen too and so they heard
all about the days when
animals strolled around just
the same as us folks.

 These are some of those
stories that Uncle Remus
told long ago.

Brer Fox was strutting around the neighbourhood feeling mighty pleased with himself. He had made good and sure that everyone, but *everyone,* had heard all about how he had tricked poor old Brer Rabbit with the sticky tar baby. Certainly Miss Meadows and her girls thought it was the funniest thing they had ever heard!

The next time Brer Rabbit came a-visiting, their stifled giggles quite ruined the conversation. Brer Rabbit drank his tea just as polite as you would wish and said not a word. But by and by, he put down his cup.

"Ladies," he announced. "Brer Fox was my daddy's riding horse for a good thirty years," then he bid them good-day and left.

Next day Brer Fox came a-calling and Miss Meadows told him what Brer Rabbit had said. Brer Fox grew quite red with anger then, composing himself, said,

"Ladies, I'm gonna make that Brer Rabbit eat his words and spit 'em out right here where you can see 'em!" and with that he headed straight for Brer Rabbit's house.

Well, Brer Rabbit wasn't at all surprised to hear Brer Fox banging on his front door but he kept as quiet as a weevil. Brer Fox hammered and hammered, blam! blam! blam! but still Brer Rabbit laid low.

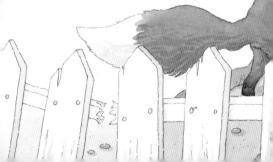

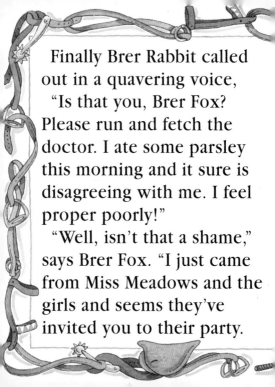

Finally Brer Rabbit called out in a quavering voice, "Is that you, Brer Fox? Please run and fetch the doctor. I ate some parsley this morning and it sure is disagreeing with me. I feel proper poorly!"

"Well, isn't that a shame," says Brer Fox. "I just came from Miss Meadows and the girls and seems they've invited you to their party.

Wouldn't be worth having a party if you couldn't be there, they said."

Then they set to arguing about whether or not Brer Rabbit was well enough to go to the party. Brer Rabbit says he can't walk there, so Brer Fox says he'll carry him. Brer Rabbit says he'll drop him so to make sure he'll be safe he must ride on the Fox's back.

Eventually after much humming and hawing Brer Fox agrees. Then Brer Rabbit says he can't ride without a saddle and Brer Fox says he'll fetch a saddle. Then Brer Rabbit says he'll fall off unless he has a bridle to hold onto and Brer Fox agrees to fetch a bridle. Oh, but it has to have blinkers, says Brer Rabbit, quite firmly.

And so Brer Fox says he'll fetch blinkers — but on one condition. Brer Rabbit cannot ride him all the way to Miss Meadows. Oh, no! That would never do. Brer Rabbit must get off and walk so no-one can see Brer Fox wearing a saddle. And so Brer Rabbit agrees and then that's all settled and off runs Brer Fox to get the saddle and bridle.

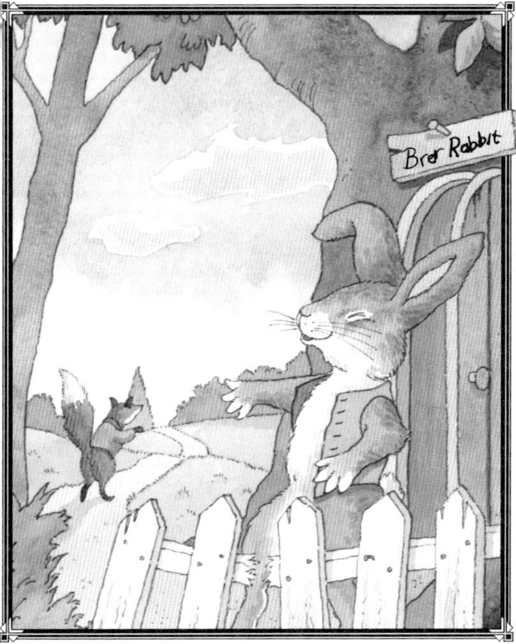
Brer Rabbit

With a big smile on his face, that Brer Rabbit gets ready for the party. He combs his hair, waxes his moustache and soon looks fine and dandy.

Up comes Brer Fox in saddle and bridle and up jumps Brer Rabbit as if he was a born horseman!

And so all was settled and off they set down the road and by and by Brer Fox felt Brer Rabbit raise one of his feet.

"I'm just shortening my left stirrup," explained the Rabbit. Soon Brer Rabbit raised his other foot.

"Just shortening my right stirrup," he told Brer Fox, but *would* you believe it, that wily Rabbit had fitted himself with spurs and now he was ready to have some fun! As they drew close to Miss Meadows' house, Brer Fox stopped, for he wanted Brer Rabbit to get off and walk, but Brer Rabbit just smiled and stuck his spurs into Brer Fox's flanks.

My, how that Fox shifted!
Past the house they
galloped, then turned and
raced back again.

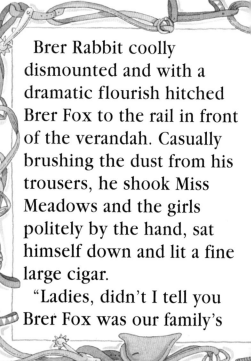

Brer Rabbit coolly dismounted and with a dramatic flourish hitched Brer Fox to the rail in front of the verandah. Casually brushing the dust from his trousers, he shook Miss Meadows and the girls politely by the hand, sat himself down and lit a fine large cigar.

"Ladies, didn't I tell you Brer Fox was our family's

riding horse? Of course, he's a bit past it now but I may be able to lick him into shape," and then they all laughed and laughed whilst poor Brer Fox tugged at the hitching rail to be free.

Brer Rabbit had tea and cakes and sang and talked for hours but finally it was time to go. He mounted Brer Fox and rode off with a gracious wave of his hand.

Off he went down the road but as soon as they were out of sight Brer Fox went wild. He bucked and pranced, snorted and cavorted but he might just as well have wrestled with his own shadow for all the good it did him. Brer Rabbit dug in those spurs and yanked on that bridle and soon Brer Fox was as mad as a bee-stung bear.

Then Brer Fox lay down on the ground and rolled on his back and in no time at all Brer Rabbit was off and running. Brer Fox chased him and very near got him, too, but Brer Rabbit made straight for a hollow tree and was soon safe and sound inside. Brer Fox lay down outside the hole and did some thinking. Soon Brer Buzzard came flopping along.

"You stand guard over this hole, Brer Buzzard," said Brer Fox, "and don't you let that pesky Brer Rabbit escape. I'm gonna get my big axe!"

When Brer Fox had gone, Brer Rabbit called out of the hole, "Brer Fox! Brer Fox! I know you're out there," said he, "and I don't care. I just wish Brer Buzzard was here, that's all."

Then Brer Buzzard tried to sound like Brer Fox.

"Why do you want Brer Buzzard?" he asked.

"Oh, nothing in particular," says Brer Rabbit. "It's just that there's the biggest grey squirrel in here and if Brer Buzzard was to come to this little hole round the other side of the tree, I'm sure I could chase that little varmint straight to him."

"You drive him out," says Brer Buzzard, all eager, "and I'll make sure that Brer Buzzard gets him!"

Then Brer Rabbit kicks up a racket and Brer Buzzard rushes round to the back of the tree and licketty-spit, out races Brer Rabbit from his hole at the front of the tree and doesn't stop running till he's safe and sound in his own home!

No matter what else you might say about Brer Rabbit's children (and some people had plenty to say, such as "pesky little critters" and "darned wabbits", but we have no time to go into that now), no matter what else you might say, those rabbits were mighty careful to do just as they were told by their mother and father.

When ole man rabbit says "scoot", they scoot, and when ole Mrs Rabbit says "scat", they scat. They kept their clothes clean and they always washed behind their ears. They were good little rabbits.

And it was a good thing that these little rabbits were good and always did as they were told because one day something happened when if they *hadn't* been good, well, that would have been the end of them, for sure. This is how it came about.

Ole Brer Fox was passing by Brer Rabbit's house and he decided he would call in and pass the time of day.

But when he knocked on the door, a little voice explained that his mother and father were not at home. "My mammy is helping old Mrs Buzzard with her quilting and my pappy is inspecting Brer Turtle's cabbage patch," he said. "Hmm!" thought Brer Fox. "*Inspecting* it, is he? More like raiding it, I'd say," but he didn't say anything.

Brer Fox peeked through the window and when he saw the fat little rabbits playing hide and seek his mouth fair began to water.

He tapped on the glass
and the little rabbits froze.

"Let me in," called Brer
Fox in a soft, wheedling
voice, "and I'll just sit and
wait for your ole daddy to
return." Soon Brer Fox was
sitting in a corner of the
room and watching the
little rabbits' noses
twitching. "Don't mind
me," he said. "You all just
carry on with your games."

But somehow the rabbits had lost interest in playing and they huddled together, their ears quivering. Brer Fox badly wanted to gobble them up but he dare not do it without some sort of good excuse. Bye and bye he saw a big stalk of sugar cane leaning against the wall. "I sure am hungry," says he. "Break me off a piece of that cane, will you?"

Well, those rabbits were brought up to be polite to visitors so they tried to do as he asked. But as much as they wrestled and sweated over that sugar cane, they could not break a piece off.

Now Brer Fox knew there isn't much else tougher in the world than sugar cane and he hoped that the rabbits would fail, for then he would have an excuse to eat them. Those little rabbits pushed and pulled but the sugar cane didn't even bend.

"Hurry up, you rabs!" cried Brer Fox. "I don't like to be kept waiting." Just then the

rabbits heard a little bird
singing on the rooftop.

"Take your toofies
and gnaw it.
Take your toofies and saw it.
Saw it and gnaw it
And then you can break it!"

Then the rabbits set to
with their sharp little teeth
and in no time at all they
laid a fine piece of juicy
sugar cane at ole Brer Fox's
feet.

Brer Fox looked pretty sick when he saw that his crafty plan had failed, and as he chewed on the cane his mind worked overtime to come up with another way to trick them. Then he caught sight of a sieve hanging on the wall.

"Here, rabbits!" he said. "I'm mighty thirsty. Take this sieve and fetch me some water from the spring."

Then the rabbits ran down and dipped the sieve into the water, but to their dismay the water trickled straight out of the holes and all over the ground.

Each time they dipped the sieve into the spring, the water ran out again and after a while the frightened rabbits began to cry. Then the little bird sang from the treetop.

*"The sieve can hold water
same as a tray
If you fill it with moss and
daub it with clay.
The Fox will get madder the
longer you stay,*

Fill it with moss and daub it with clay."

Up jumped the rabbits and they did just as the bird had told them to do. Soon the sieve did indeed hold water just as good as a tray. They carried the water back to ole Brer Fox, but when he saw that they had succeeded he was mighty mad and he ground his teeth in a regular temper.

Then he spied a large log lying in the woodpile.

"Right, you rabs," he said just a touch testily. "I'm feeling kind of chilly. Put that log on the fire and warm me up."

The rabbits put their paws
on that log and heaved and
pushed with all their might,
but would that log budge?
No, sirree, for it was a
mighty big log. Just then
they heard the bird sing.

*"Spit on your paws and tug it
and toll it.*

*Get behind it and push it and
pole it.*

*Spit on your paws and rock it
and roll it."*

So the rabbits set to and as Brer Fox gnashed his teeth, they finally got that log on the fire. Just then who should walk in but Brer Rabbit and his wife, and they were pretty surprised to see old Brer Fox sitting there looking as black as thunder. My, how the little rabs were pleased to see them, though, and they skipped for joy. Then Brer

Fox grinned sheepishly, for he saw that his game was up. He got to his feet and began to make his excuses to leave. Brer Rabbit only needed to take one look at his jittery little children to realise that something had been going on and he narrowed his eyes. "Why, do stay and have tea with us, Brer Fox. I get quite lonesome these long nights."

But Brer Fox shuffled to the door and was off.

"Thank you kindly, Brer Rabbit," says he, "but not this time — no, not this time."

Late one afternoon Brer Rabbit was on his way home after a good day rooting about in ole Brer Fox's peanut patch. As the long shadows stretched out across the dusty ground he stopped and yawned.

"What wouldn't I give for something to drink," he said to himself. Just then he spied Miss Cow grazing peacefully in the meadow.

"Something like a nice long drink of milk," he added. "Yes, that would go down a treat."

Now he knew that Miss Cow would not give him some of her milk. No, sirree. He had asked her once before and had received a less than satisfactory reply. So he would just have to think of a plan. "Howdy, Sis Cow," said Brer Rabbit, as he leaned over the fence.

"Why, howdy, Brer Rabbit," replied Miss Cow

and she carried on chewing the sweet grass.

"How's life treating you these days, Sis Cow?" says he, all polite and respectful.

"Why, fair to middling," replied Miss Cow, and she looked at him with her big brown eyes. "And how's life treating you?"

"Oh, no complaints," said Brer Rabbit. "No complaints at all."

"How's Brer Bull getting on?" asked Brer Rabbit.

"Oh, so-so, I guess," said Miss Cow. Then Brer Rabbit cleared his throat. "There are some mighty fine persimmons in that there tree, Sis Cow," says he. "I sure would like to taste some of that fruit."

Miss Cow looked up at the branches above her head.

"How are you going to

reach them?" she asked.

Brer Rabbit looked back at her, unblinkingly. "Well, I wondered if you might help me out there," he said. "If you butted the tree you could shake them to the ground." Miss Cow was happy to oblige. She ran up to the persimmon tree and banged her horns hard against the trunk — *blam!* But not a single fruit fell down. Then Miss Cow took several steps backwards, lowered her head and ran against the tree at full speed — *blim*! Not a persimmon budged from the branch. And it was hardly surprising, for those persimmons were as green as grass and nowhere near ripe enough to fall — as Brer Rabbit knew full well. Then Miss Cow backed up again.

This time she hit the tree so hard — *kerblam*! that it was a wonder she didn't knock herself out on the spot. But when she came to step away from the tree she found she couldn't move.

One of her horns had stuck in the tree and she was caught fast! She couldn't move forward, she couldn't move backward, Miss Cow was well and truly there to stay. Then Brer Rabbit smiled to himself for his plan had worked perfectly.

"Help me out, Brer Rabbit," begged Miss Cow.

"*I* won't be much help to

you, Sis Cow," he called out, "but I'll run and tell Brer Bull, if you like."

Then off he ran down the road. It wasn't long before he returned — but who was this accompanying him? It certainly didn't look like big Brer Bull! It was Brer Rabbit's missus and all Brer Rabbit's little chilluns and every one of them held a milking pail.

The big chilluns had big pails and the little chilluns had little pails and pretty soon they were clustered so tight around Miss Cow you could hardly see hide nor hair of her.

Ole Brer Rabbit calmly sat down on his three legged milking stool and filled pail after pail with sweet warm milk and pretty soon he had milked Miss Cow dry. Then he stood up and grinned.

"I realised you were gonna be stuck in that there tree all night and I figured you'd be pretty sore carrying all that milk, so I thought I'd help you out. Kind of a good deed, you might say." Then he skedaddled off down the road after his family and their clinking milk pails. Miss Cow was just beside herself with rage. All night long she tried to free herself but it wasn't until daybreak that she finally tugged her horn out of the trunk. The first thing she did was to eat some grass and fill her empty stomach.

Then she stopped to think how she might get her own back on that pesky Brer Rabbit. She reckoned he would be coming along that way soon so she stuck her horn back in the tree trunk. She had got a trick up her sleeve for sure. But that cunning Brer Rabbit returned bright and early and he saw Miss Cow push her horn back in the hole.

"Hold your horses, Sis Cow," he said to himself. "Looks to me as if you took one mouthful of grass too many. If you want to play tricks on me, you gotta be quicker than that." Then he came loping up the road whistling a merry tune and looking the very picture of innocence. "Morning, Sis Cow," he said, "and how are you this fine morning?"

"Oh, proper poorly," says she with a groan. "Try as I might, I just can't pull my horn free from his tree."

"Why, I'm real unhappy to hear that, Sis Cow," said Brer Rabbit. "Can I be of any assistance to you?"

"Why, I reckon if you stood behind me and caught hold of my tail and pulled real hard, why, you might just pull that horn free."

So Brer Rabbit sauntered up to Miss Cow and stood just a little way off. "Reckon I'm close enough here," he said. "I'm only a puny little fellow and I sure don't want to get trampled under your hard hooves." Miss Cow twitched her tail angrily. "That ain't no use at all," says she. "You aren't nearly close enough to pull my tail." Then Brer Rabbit just smiles kinda slow. "You do the pulling, Sis Cow, and I'll do your grunting for you." Well, Miss Cow was so mad that Brer Rabbit could have sworn he saw real steam coming out of her nostrils. With a loud moo, she pulled her horn from the hole as if from butter and she was off down the meadow just inches behind ole Brer Rabbit's heels.

Down the road scorched
Brer Rabbit with his ears
laid flat down the back of
his head, and after him
thundered Miss Cow in hot
pursuit.

Suddenly Brer Rabbit saw a handy briar patch and in he jumped. Round the corner came Miss Cow and she skidded to a halt. Brer Rabbit stuck his head out and his eyes were as big and as round as two of Miss Meadows' best saucers.

"Hello, Sis Cow!" called Brer Rabbit in a squeaky voice. "Where are you heading in such a hurry?"

"Did you see Brer Rabbit, Brer Big-Eyes?" she asked.

"He ran past just a minute ago," said Brer Rabbit, and with that Miss Cow charged off down the road and Brer Rabbit just lay back in that briar patch and laughed till his sides ached.

Brer Fox was after him, Brer Buzzard was after him, Sis Cow was after him — but they hadn't caught him yet!

JOEL CHANDLER HARRIS

The *Brer Rabbit* stories began as American
Negro fables, told by the slaves working on
plantations in the deep South of North America,
and almost certainly African in origin.
Joel Chandler Harris (1848-1908) insisted that
he did no more than simply retell the
stories, but in fact he showed great storytelling
skill in padding out what was often little more
than a folk saying. He also retained the
wonderfully rich dialect of the southern Negro
slaves, writing the words just as they would
have been said. This text has been adapted for
easier reading and understanding, but still
retains the flavour of Uncle Remus's relaxed
storytelling style.